Wink

THE NINJA WHO WANTED TO BE NOTICED

BY J. C. PHILLIPPS

VIKING

It was the happiest day of Wink's life when he was accepted to the Summer Moon School for Young Ninjas.

Master Zutsu taught the students to be strong and practice the art of stealth.

"Silence is the weapon of the ninja," Master Zutsu said.

But Wink could not be silent.

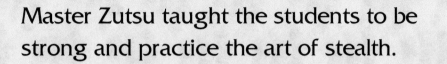

"Look at me!" he hollered.

Master Zutsu clapped like thunder and raised one angry finger to his lips.

Later, the ninjas practiced their positions.

"Roundhouse kick!" Master Zutsu ordered.

One by one, the young ninjas performed.

And then there was Wink.

YAHOO!

Master Zutsu's face twitched.

"The loudest cricket is the first to be caught."

He sent Wink home.

Grandmother greeted him.

"You look so sad, Wink-chan. The Lucky Dragon Circus has come. Let us go and regain your smile."

Wink sank into a pillow.

"Ninjas are stealthy and silent," he answered. "They don't go to the circus."

"Time spent laughing is time well spent," Grandmother said.

Wink said nothing and stared at the curtains. *Those are nice and bright,* he thought.

The next day, Master Zutsu sent the students into a field. "A ninja can disappear in any landscape," he said.

The young ninjas became waving blades of grass, blending into the countryside.

Then there was Wink.

Master Zutsu frowned. "The blossom that flaunts its color is soon plucked!"

"But I'm being stealthy," Wink argued. "I didn't make a sound."

"Silent to the ear, invisible to the eye—that is the art of stealth," Master Zutsu proclaimed. He sent Wink home.

Grandmother poured him
barley tea.

"Wink-chan, you look so
serious."

Wink sat down and sighed.

"Sometimes a worry must rest," she said. "Let us go to the circus. The acrobats will cheer you."

"Ninjas have no use for cheer," Wink replied.

He drank his tea and left the room. The next day, he would try harder.

On a field trip to the zoo, Wink saw a chance to make Master Zutsu proud. He climbed into the panda's pen and hid among the bamboo.

Yahoo! Wink thought. *No one sees me. I'm super stealthy. I'm the greatest ninja in all the world!*

But if no one sees me, no one knows I'm super stealthy.

No one knows I'm a great ninja.

He couldn't help it.
Wink just wanted
to be noticed.

Master Zutsu didn't say anything.

He raised one arm and extended a long, bony finger.

Wink walked away with his head hanging. How could he show Master Zutsu he was a good ninja?

From the other side of the wall he heard a loud

CLANK!

A boy was busy stacking boards and cans.

"What are you doing?" Wink asked.

"Practicing," said the boy.

He climbed on top of his stack and
tried to stand but fell over with a thud.

"Your legs are too stiff," Wink said.
"Knees bend like the breeze.
Hips become strong like rocks."

Wink sprang to the top to demonstrate.

The boy's family watched and clapped.

"Well done!" said the father.

A smile spread across Wink's face.
"I can do more!"

So Wink came back the next day, and the next, and the next, and showed the boy and his family all the things he could do.

"He moves like a gazelle—swift and graceful," the mother said.

"His spirit shines like the morning sun," added the father.

One day, both Master Zutsu and Wink's grandmother received special envelopes in the mail.

Inside each was a ticket . . .

. . . to the Lucky Dragon Circus!

"Ladies and gentlemen, I am honored to present . . .

THE NIMBLE NINJA!"

Wink burst into view, flying through the air like a glittering cannonball.

He did ax kicks, fist strikes, hook punches, reverse chops,

crescent kicks, iron palms, and front and back tornado flips.

He even juggled fire sticks while balancing on a shoot of bamboo.

Wink took a bow, and the audience clapped and cheered.

Grandmother said, "Your smile has come home."

Master Zutsu said, "Free-flowing water will always find its way."

And then there was Wink.

Wink didn't say anything.

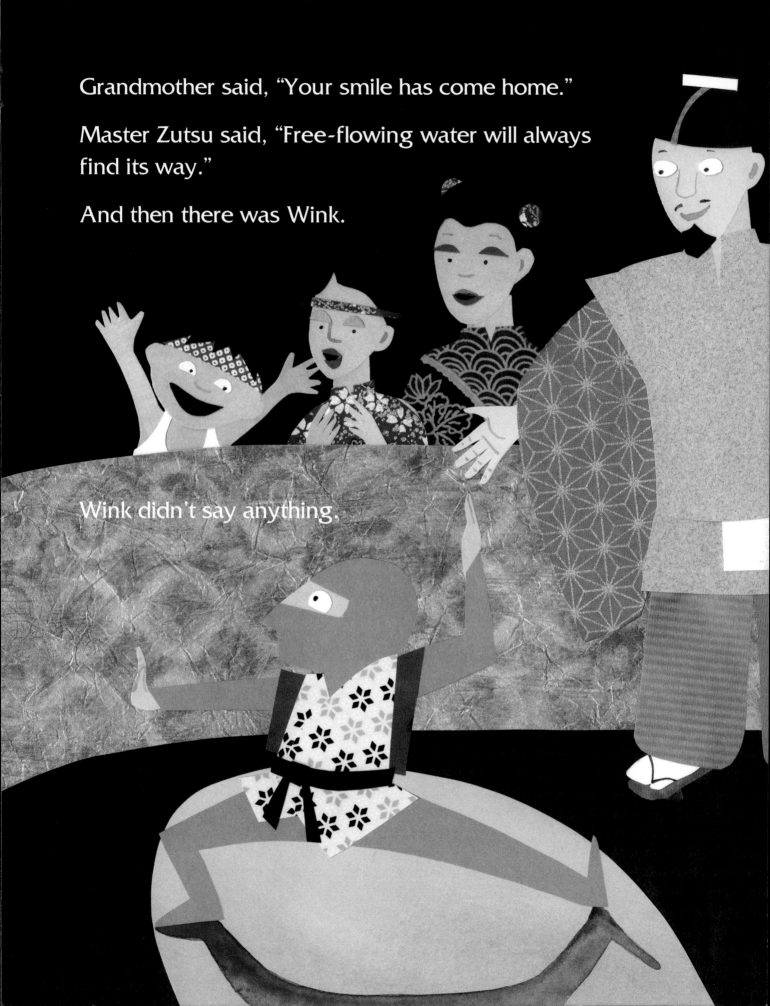

He smiled and took another bow.

For Cameron and Jon, next-door ninjas

VIKING
Published by Penguin Group
Penguin Young Readers Group, 345 Hudson Street, New York, New York 10014, U.S.A.
Penguin Group (Canada), 90 Eglinton Avenue East, Suite 700, Toronto, Ontario, Canada M4P 2Y3
(a division of Pearson Penguin Canada Inc.)
Penguin Books Ltd, 80 Strand, London WC2R 0RL, England
Penguin Ireland, 25 St Stephen's Green, Dublin 2, Ireland (a division of Penguin Books Ltd)
Penguin Group (Australia), 250 Camberwell Road, Camberwell, Victoria 3124, Australia
(a division of Pearson Australia Group Pty Ltd)
Penguin Books India Pvt Ltd, 11 Community Centre, Panchsheel Park, New Delhi – 110 017, India
Penguin Group (NZ), 67 Apollo Drive, Rosedale, North Shore 0632, New Zealand
(a division of Pearson New Zealand Ltd)
Penguin Books (South Africa) (Pty) Ltd, 24 Sturdee Avenue, Rosebank, Johannesburg 2196, South Africa

First published in 2009 by Viking, a division of Penguin Young Readers Group

3 5 7 9 10 8 6 4

Copyright © J. C. Phillipps, 2009

LIBRARY OF CONGRESS CATALOGING-IN-PUBLICATION DATA
Phillipps, J. C. (Julie)
Wink: The ninja who wanted to be noticed / by J.C. Phillipps.
p. cm.
Summary: Although ninjas should be silent with stealth, Wink finds his enthusiasm gets
him into trouble with his teacher until he finds the perfect way to express both emotions.
ISBN 978-0-670-01092-9 (hardcover)
[1. Ninja—Fiction. 2. Schools—Fiction. 3. Japan—Fiction.] I. Title.
PZ7.P53725Wi 2009
[E]—dc22
2008023238

Manufactured in China
Set in Alliance